Down in the dumps with the

Nasty Gnarlies

(Featuring Snooty Judy Butterfly)

Keith Graves

Scholastic Press — New York

Graves, Keith. Three nasty gnarlies / by Keith Graves.— 1st ed. p. cm. Summary:
In an effort to improve their cleanliness and appearance, three nasty gnarlies follow a
butterfly's advice. • ISBN 0-439-24090-5 • [1. Cleanliness— Fiction. 2. Self-perception—
Fiction. 3. Self-esteem— Fiction. 4. Butterflies— Fiction. 5. Stories in rhyme.]
I. Title. PZ8.3.G74243 Th 2003 [E]— dc21 2002070788
10 9 8 7 6 5 4 3 2 1   03 04 05 06 07
Printed in Singapore 46 • First edition, November 2003 • The type was set
in P22 Daddy-O Hip. The display type was handlettered by Keith Graves.
The music was transcribed by Jessica Bruder and typeset by Randa
Kirschbaum. The art for this book was rendered in acrylic
paint on illustration board. • Book design by
Yvette Awad and Marijka Kostiw

For Max,
nastiest
Gnarly
of them all

(and I mean
that in a
good way).

Three Nasty Gnarlies

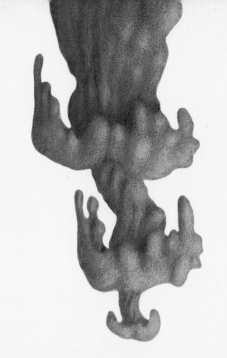

Perched atop a clump

Practicing a gnarly tune

Heard throughout the dump.

Grubby Gurgle sang soprano,

Stanky Stoo sang bass,

Ooga-Mooga stomped her feet

And yodeled just in case.

"Oh, we are Nasty Gnarlies.

We like to make a mess.

Getting stuck in yucky muck

Is what we like the best!

"We're fabulously smelly,

Like pungent potpourri.

What could be more beautiful

Than nasty gnarly we?"

But Snooty Judy Butterfly

Heard their happy song.

"Did someone mention beauty?"

She sniffed. "You've got it wrong!

"You Gnarlies are not beautiful.

You exude a rank bouquet.

You're untidy, and your style

Is oh so très passé!"

"You mean I'm stinky?" Stanky gasped.

"I never would have guessed!"

"I'm not gorgeous?" Grubby cried.

"I'm a lumpy, frumpy mess?"

Simply
PEW,
darling!

Most
uncouth!

Rather
dreary,
dearie.

Ooga-Mooga drooled and sobbed,

And chewed her favorite shoe.

The Nasty Gnarlies begged for help.

"Oh, pooh! I've hurt your feelings.

But things are not so bleak.

You simply need to spiffy up!

I'll show you my technique.

"Though I am now exquisite,

PERFECT, I confess,

Once I was a muddy worm,

A peasant bug no less."

"No. No. It was quite easy.

I wrapped myself in silk.

When springtime came, I flew away —

My body was rebuilt."

ta-ta!

So snooty Judy said goodbye

To the grateful grungy three.

Then each one said, "It worked for HER —
But will it work for ME?"

They wrapped
themselves in
bits of junk
And dangled
from the trees.
They slept
and dreamt
of butterflies
floating in
the breeze.

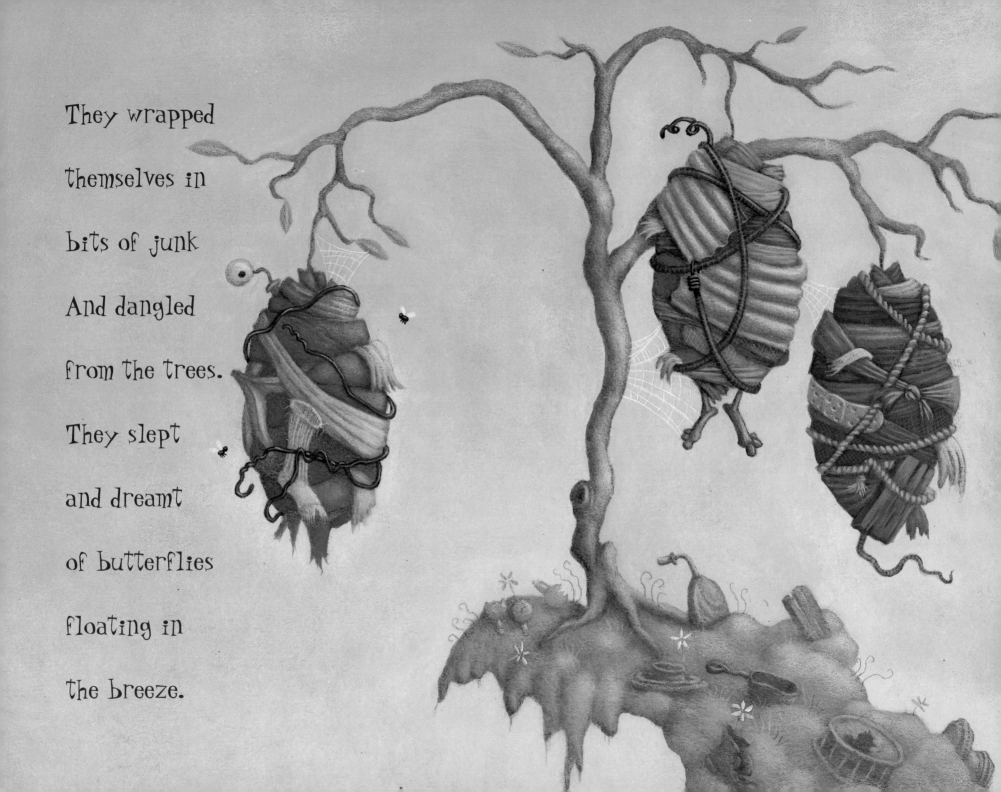

Then one day in early May, Gurgle wriggled free.

Next came Stoo, then Ooga-Mooga fell out of the tree.

"Oh, look at us! We're butterflies!

So dainty and petite."

They flapped their arms and tried to fly,

Then plopped down in a heap.

"Something's wrong,"

said Stanky Stoo

With sorrow in his eyes.

"The beauty treatment failed

To make us metamorphosize!"

"We don't look like Judy!"

The grimy trio shrieked.

"There's no beauty in our bodies —

No suave on our physiques!"

Then Ooga-Mooga had a thought.

"Could Judy have it wrong?

"Our beauty **IS** our gnarliness.

We were pretty all along!"

"I like that thought," said Grubby.

"Our funk is quite divine!

I don't want to be a butterfly,

I'd rather bathe in slime!"

"I gotta be **ME!**" sang Stanky,

"My gnarly fumes are strong!

We're nastier than ever now.

Let's sing our favorite song!"

"Oh, we are Nasty Gnarlies.
We're dirty and we reek.
We're gloopy-gloppy-glamorous.
We're positively chic.
Grubby, Stanky, Ooga-Mooga,
Rolling in stromboli,
Rocka, rumba, floobie flow,
Nocka wocka moly."

And though the Nasty Gnarlies

Are Nasty Gnarlies still,

They see themselves as beautiful

As summer daffodils.